Mooresville Public Library
304 South Main
Mooresville, NC
Ph (704)-664-2

D0593235

Mooresville Public Library
304 South Main St.
Mooresville, NC 28115
Ph (704)-664-2927

WITHDRAWN

Tadpoles

The Hungry Little Monkey

by Andy Blackford

Illustrated by Gabriele Antonini

Crabtree Publishing Company

www.crabtreebooks.com

Crabtree Publishing Company

www.crabtreebooks.com
1-800-387-7650

616 Welland Ave.
St. Catharines, ON
L2M 5V6

PMB 59051, 350 Fifth Ave.
59th Floor,
New York, NY

Published by Crabtree Publishing in 2011

Series Editor: Jackie Hamley
Editors: Melanie Palmer, Reagan Miller
Series Advisor: Catherine Glavina
Series Designer: Peter Scoulding
Project Coordinator: Kathy Middleton
Print and production coordinator: Katherine Berti

Text © Andy Blackford 2010
Illustration © Gabriele Antonini 2010

Printed in Canada/042011/KR20110304

All rights reserved. No part
of this publication may be
reproduced, stored in a retrieval
system, or transmitted in any
form or by any means, electronic,
mechanical, photocopy, recording
or otherwise, without the prior
written permission of the
copyright owner.

First published in 2010
by Franklin Watts
(A division of Hachette
Children's Books)

The rights of the author and the
illustrator of this Work have
been asserted.

**Library and Archives Canada
Cataloguing in Publication**

Blackford, Andy
 The hungry little monkey / by Andy Blackford ;
illustrated by Gabriele Antonini.

(Tadpoles)
ISBN 978-0-7787-0581-9 (bound).--
ISBN 978-0-7787-0592-5 (pbk.)

  I. Antonini, Gabriele II. Title. III. Series: Tadpoles
(St. Catharines, Ont.)

PZ10.3.B52Hu 2011   j823'.92   C2011-900156-X

**Library of Congress
Cataloging-in-Publication Data**

Blackford, Andy.
 The hungry little monkey / by Andy Blackford ;
illustrated by Gabriele Antonini.
  p. cm. -- (Tadpoles)
 Summary: Little Monkey is very hungry, but none of
the other jungle animals seems able to tell him how to
peel and eat his banana.
 ISBN 978-0-7787-0592-5 (pbk. : alk. paper) -- ISBN
978-0-7787-0581-9 (reinforced library binding : alk. paper)
 [1. Bananas--Fiction. 2. Monkeys--Fiction. 3. Jungle animals
--Fiction.] I. Antonini, Gabriele, ill. II. Title. III. Series.

PZ7.B53228Hun 2011
[E]--dc22

                                           2010052367

Here is a list of the words in this story.
Common words:

a	he	mom	that
asked	it	not	was
at	little	said	
for	looked		

Other words:

banana	monkey	squeeze
bite	parrot	suck
did	peck	tiger
hungry	peel	work
lion		yum

Little Monkey
was hungry.

3

He asked for a banana.

He looked at it.

"Bite it!" said Tiger.

8

That did not work.

9

"Peck it!" said Parrot.

11

That did not work.

"Suck it!" said Lion.

14

15

That did not work.

"Squeeze it!" said Snake.

18

That did not work.

"Peel it!" said Mom.

"Yum!" said Little Monkey.

Puzzle Time

Can you find these
pictures in the story?

Which pages are
the pictures from?

Answers

The pictures come from these pages:
a. pages 12 and 13
b. pages 6 and 7
c. pages 16 and 17
d. pages 10 and 11

Notes for adults

Tadpoles are structured to provide support for early readers. The stories may also be used by adults for sharing with young children.

Starting to read alone can be daunting. **Tadpoles** help by listing the words in the book for a preview before reading. **Tadpoles** also provide strong visual support and repeat words and phrases. These books will both develop confidence and encourage reading and rereading for pleasure.

If you are reading this book with a child, here are a few suggestions:

1. Make reading fun! Choose a time to read when you and the child are relaxed and have time to share the story.

2. Look at the picture on the front cover and read the blurb on the back cover. What might the story be about? Why might the child like it?

3. Look at the list of words on page two. Can the child identify most of the words?

4. Encourage the child to retell the story using the jumbled picture puzzle on pages 22-23.

5. Discuss the story and see if the child can relate it to his or her own experiences, or perhaps compare it to another story he or she knows.

6. Give praise! Children learn best in a positive environment.

If you enjoyed this book, why not try another **TADPOLES** story?
Please see the back cover for more **TADPOLES** titles.
Visit **www.crabtreebooks.com** for other **Crabtree** books.